the lady & the thing

I wish I'd never written this.

I wish I'd never dreamed up this story, my third full attempt at the eulogy I wish I'd never needed to write, for another member of the Club No One Wants to Be In. The Lady didn't do things by halves so neither have I. She will be in the British Library now for ever, which has pushed this unexpected author, illustrator and bereaved unbiological little sister to finish this book, for her babies, and all our babies that might need to know about her. It is more work of heart than art- how it should be.

Eulogies spoken, even unusual ones scribbled furiously by another dying persons' bedside, read aloud to so many different people, fade with time and people's memories. It may not be professional, award winning or sit on shelves in shops. It may never grace anyone's shelves but mine and her closest friends and family. I didn't expect to do life without her, but can rest a little easier knowing she is still helping people.

With thanks to:
Bloom Gin "Bloom Bright" competition whose winnings purchased the tools I needed
WSX Enterprise for their wise advice and grant to create a website.
Frank Turner for our anthem, his lyrics, soundtrack to my 2021 (& kind permission to use his lyrics)
Nana Lee who was the first person to hear this story whilst I scribbled at her bedside,
but most of all, Rich and Doris for letting me tell her tale.

Special thanks to Bosom Pals Southend
who made a scribbled story a real life children's book and continued Faye's legacy.

Thank you!

THE LADY  & THE THING

by Laura King

For Amelia and Imogen
I promised your Mummy I'd love you both fiercely, always.
I hope this story shines a light on how special she is,
and how loved you are.
With love,
Aunty Laura xxx

Dear Faye
My unbiological big sister who inspired this story.
*"Messy **is** more beautiful than perfect"*
Love you infinitely, too.
LJ xxx

ISBN 978-173965260-9

9 781739 652609

Published in 2022 by Little Light Publishing Limited
First edition (paperback)

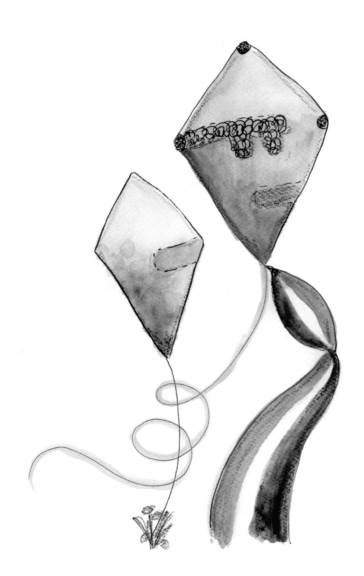

One day a Lady found a Thing, hiding in her chest.
She took it to the doctor, to see what they thought best.

They said, *"we need to study it to learn about it more"*

The Lady said,

"please tell me, I beseech you, I implore!"

The Thing was very, very rare, but not rare like a treasure
The Lady said, *"but just how bad? I'd really like the measure"*

The doctors and the nurses, technicians and the lab
They looked and looked, prodded and poked,

But thought,

"hmm, this looks bad"

*"This is a very Bad Thing, we're sorry to bring the news
But this Thing will make you very sick unless it is removed"*

You see, the Lady is a mummy.
A wife and daughter, too.

She went straight home to tell them
what they were going to do.

The naughty Thing took lots of stuff to try and make it shrink.

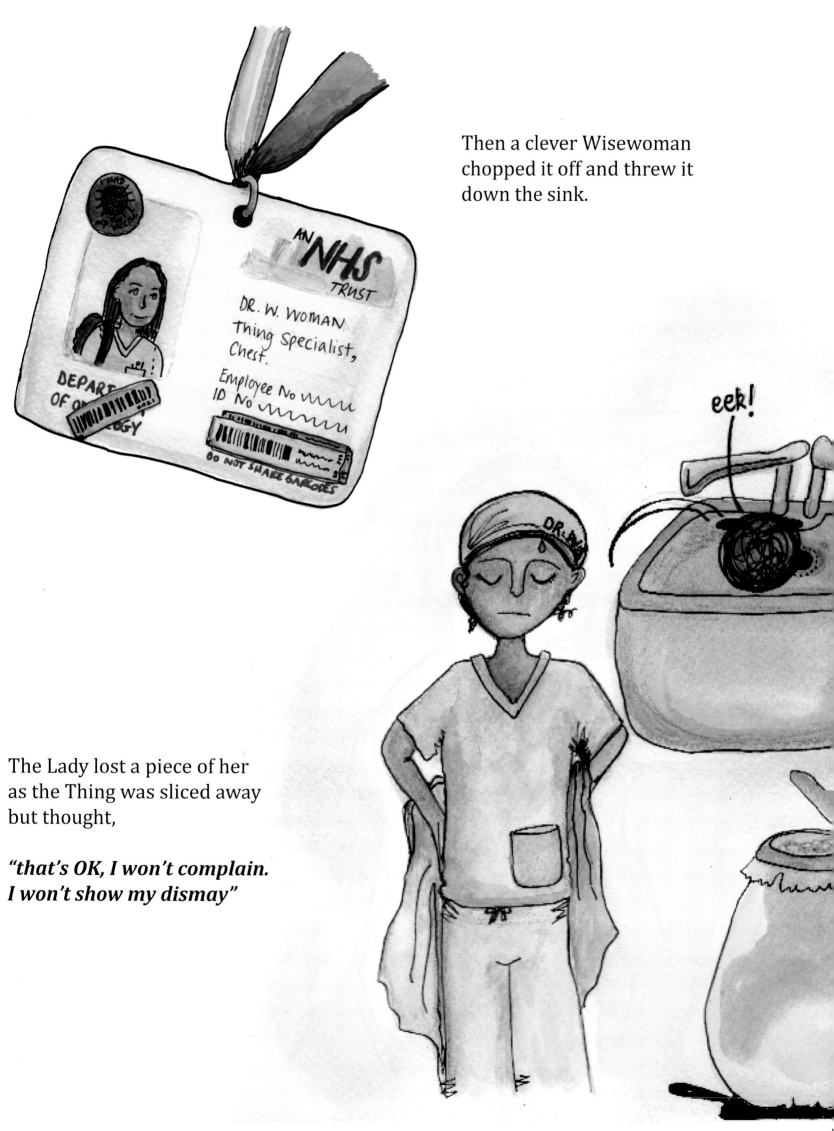

Then a clever Wisewoman chopped it off and threw it down the sink.

The Lady lost a piece of her as the Thing was sliced away but thought,

"that's OK, I won't complain. I won't show my dismay"

You see, the Lady's very special because she chose to see the joy

in living with the bad Thing's pain and the parts the Thing destroys

She had to look quite different,
wigs and hats, just like a crown.

Although inside she was scared,
she tried hard not to frown

The Wisewoman gave her armour
They used lots of lasers, too

The Thing got

smaller
smaller
smaller

MEGA LASER 500

Everyone sighed,

"phew!"

!

Meanwhile, the Lady felt its presence behind her like a shadow.
She tried hard not to notice, to try and let it go.

But...

One day the Thing, it showed itself. It had come back once again

She said, "You beast! How dare you return when we feel normal again"

"Supercalifragilisticexpialidocious"

Once again it was removed, but this time at a cost.
The Lady broke more bits of her and her chest was
lost. She liked things to be symmetrical, so it really
was quite tricky. The scars and missing bits and pieces made her feel quite icky.

"Three cheers, HOORAY!" everyone cried,

and once again said,

"PHEW!"

Because of another **Awful Thing**, they touched elbows, too.

The Lady felt quite funny, because whilst the
Thing was gone, she felt its presence every day.
Every.

Single.

One.

Like a highwayman by the road,
she worried they would meet, shouting

*"HA, HA, HA,
I got you twice, and thrice would be a treat!"*

And she was right,

and back it came.

It **crept back** with no noise.

But this time it was somewhere else
and it couldn't be **destroyed.**

She went back to the Wisewoman. Big teams, professors too-
They spoke of

SUPER MEGA LASERS,

magic potions new.

But, Things moving somewhere else was rare. There wasn't much to do.

She wrote it down, what Things looked like, how it felt and it behaved.
She typed and typed,
and many different people
read her page.

"Gut feelings are our guardian angels"

"GIVE ME A BREAK!"

"together we are our own STRONG GIRLS' CLUB"

The Lady, she was very brave and strong, and kind, and caring.
The Thing, it needed studying. How to find it needed sharing.

Because of her bravery and truth she told, others found their Thing and checked their chests. It really made a difference to know where Things hid best.

They sang out,

"Why thank you, Lady. You're honest and you're brave.
Even though your Thing won't budge, many others you will save"

The Lady was so tired, in pain from constant battles.
She took so many potions and pills, she thought one day she'd rattle.

But she took the Thing and hugged it close
"I'll embrace you now, wild Thing

Because you are part of me now,

and I'll not let you win"

She took her time left with the Thing, she carried it around.
She told everyone she loved, how much.

Her people felt so proud.

The people who loved her made a pot.
It was filled with glittering gold
To try to make memories her babies
would remember 'til they're old.

She carried the Thing round with her still, as she spread her love and cheer.
Wherever she went, she left some love for the people she held most dear.

She inked a hug button on her skin
so her babies felt her near,
and spent the time crafting kindly gifts
for when she wasn't here.

She left some people tasks to do,
like any clever mother.
Some of them were little gifts,
some to care for others.

You see, she knew just what would happen
(she knew it from the start)
and whilst it made her furious...

The Thing thought,
" why embrace me?
it really is quite
curious"

The Lady said,

"well, you see, Thing, you're trying to spread sadness

and whilst I walk upon the Earth,
I want to feel just *gladness*"

"With my time left, I want to spread kindness and love for miles
so when I'm gone in body, I'll be thought of with huge smiles"

So many people loved the Lady, from places far and wide
(they were all very different, on the outside and inside).

They shouted,
"this just isn't fair!"

-- Some did swear and curse,
**_"our lovely Lady, kind and caring,
so many poorly children nursed"_**

♪ *"you'll live to dance another day - it's just now you
have to dance for the two of us ... So STOP
looking so damn DEPRESSED, and sing
with all your
HEART ..."** *FRANK TURNER, LONG LIVE THE QUEEN ♫ (permission given)

But the Lady took them one by one,
and one by one she said,

**_"this Thing, it is quite frightening
and I don't want you to be scared"_**

There's sunshine to be found when skies are stormy and just seem grey.
Because love, it lasts forever, that means it never goes away,

And when you're feeling sad or glum you can embrace the storm

"*Because*", the Lady said, "*my friendship keeps you warm*"

"*Love is like a string*",

she said,

"*it ties us all together*"

"*and love on strings can keep us close and
weather any weather*"

The Lady gently **left the Earth.**
She'd tried to stay with all her might.

It was **bravery** that let her go,
when she was tired of the fight.

She left her body peaceful there, but she left her strings tied **tight**
Her strings to her two babies are the ones that shine
most **bright...**

Heroes actually walk with us
each and every day:

some discover,

some blaze trails,

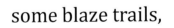

and some take pain away

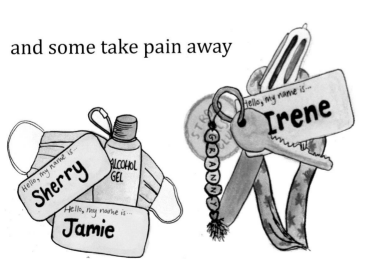

Now everywhere she walked, there springs up a little flower, from the Earth, reminding us

kindness is a superpower.

The End.

The Lady

This Lady's real name was Faye. She was a wife, daughter, sister, auntie, mummy to two girls and all round goodie. She was human -implusive, sweary, and very, very blunt. She was also a children's nurse, working in palliative care. Her patients and families adored her. Because of her job, she had a dark sense of humour and strongly believed in telling kids the truth, however unpalatable, in a way that made sense to them. When her cancer returned for the first time, she started journalling and wrote a blog called Return of the Beast. This helped her process her diagnosis, reaching many fellow women in her position, but was also a way for her to share her journey.

The Thing

In this instance, the Thing was triple negative breast cancer which returned twice, finally with brain metastasis. However, the story was written purposefully to be vague, to work alongside a child's imagination and hopefully shine a light on a really really difficult issue - on a subject we all hope we never have to broach. Sometimes we have to, and sometimes you need something a bit unusual to do that.

I like details...

One of the things Faye was a passionate advocate for was ensuring her children knew enough to understand, and deal with her diagnosis- but in a way that was appropriate and supportive.

She would have approved of visually gaining weight, becoming bald and essentially becoming unrecognisable – because this is what happened.

I am proud to say that whilst we are not biologically siblings, she was my big sister in all the ways that matter. I am not proud to say that at one point even I didn't recognise her when it had been a while due to the COVID19 pandemic.

Whilst she didn't see this book, because it was my eulogy, I feel strongly that she would have liked details to be recognisable to children, to normalise what is happening and aid & facilitate conversation around what is happening or may happen, even with small children. So, the Lady has a syringe driver, she has accurate medicines on her shelf, it isn't a fairytale ending, or religious. She was sweary and blunt, so it needed to be the antithesis of fluffy.
  --- and yes, she was totally, utterly, entirely fed up!!!

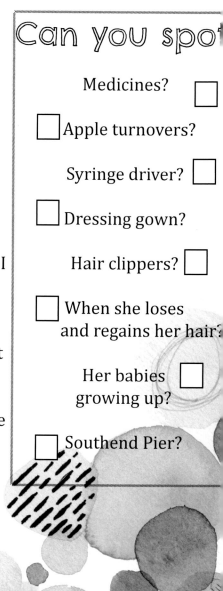

Can you spot

Medicines? ☐

☐ Apple turnovers?

Syringe driver? ☐

☐ Dressing gown?

Hair clippers? ☐

☐ When she loses and regains her hair?

Her babies ☐ growing up?

☐ Southend Pier?